2018 Young Writers To Follow

Escambia, Okaloosa and
Santa Rosa County
Middle and High Schools

Printed in the United States of America

First Printing, **2018**

Proper Publishing
P.O. Box 634
Cantonment, FL 32533
www.properpublishing.info
theproperpublisher@yahoo.com

Cover photo courtesy:
Pixabay

Acknowledgments:

Thank you to the teachers and school administrators of Escambia, Okaloosa and Santa Rosa Counties for providing students the information about this publication.

Thank you to the West Florida Literary Federation for introducing Mrs. Lewis to the concept of Student Poetry Contests, which has been the catalyst for this publication.

And thank you to all of the students. Without your work, and your passion for exploring words, there would be no future for the art of story-telling.

Dedication:

There are moments in your life when you are certain of your future as it appears clearly stretched out before you.

This book is dedicated to those rare moments. And to all of the young men and women who dare to overcome.

Be true to you at all times.

Contents

Tempest Makey
Fort Walton Beach High School
10th Grade, Amy Holt

25 lines from suicide notes and love letters...

1 — i love you
2 — im really sorry about, well…me i guess
3 — i knew this day was coming
4 — i promise you you're truly wonderful
5 — im sorry
6 — i keep seeing you in my dreams
7 — in 2015 i broke my ankle three separate times
8 — every time i think of the moment you read this my heart races
9 — drunk me loves you even more than sober me and i had no idea that was possible
10 — im sorry
11 — its really sad that you're so unhappy, i know what its like
12 — ill never admit it but i wish you were here with me
13 — sometimes im scared ill run out of reasons to keep talking to you
14 — when i was in forth grade i blew out my eardrum my and i can hear out of it now but its still all fuzzy fuzzy
15 — im…im sorry
16 — i miss you as soon as i leave

17 — i miss you
18 — i miss you
19 — i miss you
20 — im sorry
21 — please
22 — don't leave me too
23 — i think im serious this time
24 — im really gonna miss you
25 — im sorry

Lori Miller
J. M. Tate High School
11th Grade, Karen MacDonald

Shadow

The paranoia of always being followed.
It creeps silently, waiting to strike.
Only around during the hours of light,
cowering in the night.
Like the taste of thick chimney soot on your
tongue.
Smelling like the fumes industrial factories.
Always behind you without a second thought.

Tom Rahn
Niceville Senior High School
10th Grade, Kim Escoffier

Equality

We are all the same until race disconnects us, religion separates us, politics divide us, and wealth classifies us. Until gender, age, likes and dislikes separate us. We tell everyone we don't care who they are or what they look like, but we do care. The first thing we do when we see someone new is start deciding things about them just based off looks. We categorize everything whether it be objects, opinions, or people. We decide right away if we like or dislike them. If we want to know more about them or if we want to avoid them.

I do not believe in equality. Everyone has different needs, different wants, different lives. We can't act like a 10-year-old female born with autism is the same as a 90-year-old male who can't even use the bathroom by himself. No one is equal even if they are the same age and gender, they will have lived through different things and therefore need different lifestyles. Best friends have different wants and needs. Everyone does.

Now you might say, "Well we're all human, so we all have the same basic needs." This is true. We all need food, water, shelter, etc. If we saw people in these ways, and broke people down into the very basics then there would be no individuality. Without individuality we are all clones, we do as everyone else does and nothing makes us different. If we view things this way then no one would ever create anything new. No one would ever take a risk, or go on an adventure. There would be no point to history because it would all be the same.

So what about together, but different? What if we worked together as one, but each brought a different skill, personality trait, point of view to the table? What if we brought different thought processes from people who were raised in different communities who thought different together? By doing this we could be at what I believe to be societies best. This would make it so that everyone was represented, and everyone had a voice.

The Pledge of allegiance says "Indivisible with liberty and justice for all" written in 1892, 26 years after the 13th amendment was made, is wrong. We are divisible, we are divided into groups of race, age, sexuality. We are divided, and at the time the pledge was written people were still heavily divided by race. The Pledge also says "under god" I believe this just makes the pledge even more invalid by the fact that not everyone believes in god. People who do believe in god don't all believe in the same god.

Our country is not equal, by who everyone is and by the groups they are in. But we must use that to make us stronger not to take us apart. We must disagree on many things, but in also disagreeing we must listen to why others don't agree with us. We must come together as a whole instead of using differences to pull us apart.

Caleb Kimes
J. M. Tate High School
11th Grade, Karen MacDonald

The Golden Senses

Gold is gold

Gold can be a coin in your pocket

Gold is the taste of excellence

Like having a meal after winning a game

Gold is the shine of a golden bar

Like the iridescent puddle

Gold is chains

Clinking on your neck

Gold is the smell of joy

Like getting paid

Tramendus Hollins
J. M. Tate High School
11th Grade, Karen MacDonald

My brand new toy is a sad soul

My brand new toy is a sad soul

I saw it in the vacant lot

The substandard appearance was awful

While my parents enjoyed the humility,

my heart pounded in anger

My brand new car wasn't brand new after all

Kayla Craft
J. M. Tate High School
11th Grade, Karen MacDonald

Welcome to Tate

Welcome to Tate. Be our students. Pay attention.
Pick an elective. Hope for the best.
Get good grades. Do this do that. Be this be that.
Do it perfect. Sit there raise your hand.
Don't talk until you are called on. Is that a phone?
You have detention. Is that a phone again?
Now it's a referral. Here is a test.
You have to get a perfect grade. But,
I'm not that smart to learn it in a day,
teacher thinks we have the same brain,
know the same stuff, learn the same way.
Why go to school if we don't use this stuff.
We don't learn things we need to know.
It's not easy sitting in a classroom all day.
Trying to pay attention, getting good grades.
Maybe there is a trap door under me.
Most people want to have a life and explore.
I'm sorry I'm like fish and can't climb trees.
I wish I was all the animals and do everything.
Learn as you wish, do as you please.
But I'm a Tater and will do my best.

Cassidy Bassett

Fort Walton Beach High School
12th Grade, Lynne Shirley

The Wall

No. They are being absurd. I will stay.

The wind picked up. The wall moved closer.

This always happens. The walls approach and leave like windows of opportunity in life. They always pass. Everyone overreacts, but I never do. What is there to overreact to? Oh no, the clouds are crying. Oh no, the sun is hiding. Oh no, the heavens are screaming their ghostly wails that no one can understand. If they are not understandable, then do not listen. It is simple as that. Yet everyone tries, and they are so surprised when they discover the heavens were only fooling them with their twisted antics that only the gullible could possibly fall for. This is just another window. Nothing that I would ever spend my precious time worrying about.

But why did everyone leave? The question befuddles me. They somehow believed the lies they were fed by the media. This wall is deleterious. Please do not stay for this wall. You will regret it.

No. They are being ridiculous. I will stay.

The rain picked up. The wall moved closer.
Closer.

My window is shaking. The constant pap-pap-pap of the rain on the glass is the only sound I hear. Pap-Pap-Pap. More rain. PAP-PAP-PAP. The only sound I hear.

How did the wall get here so fast? It should have taken longer. I thought it would have taken much longer. Why was I not right? I am always right.

No. They are being stupid. I will stay.

The storm picks up. The wall is here. Here. Here.

Thunder shakes my house. I feel the foundation vibrate under my feet. It shakes and quakes and rumbles with trouble, but still. Nothing to worry about.

Right?

I can't hear anything. Is the pap-pap-pap the rain or just the buffer in my head? I can't tell the difference anymore. Occasional booms crack my mind in half. They make me dizzy. Dizzy.

Pap-Pap-CRACK. What happened to the —
BOOM.

Where did this water — BOOM.

Where did the wind — BOOM.

I can't think. My thoughts are the clouds, overlapping, combining, crossing, leaping, jumping, crawling, screaming, black.

My skin is cold. Cold. Cold.

My toes are numb. Numb. Numb?

My mind is blank. Blank. Blank!

The water's in my house! House!

What do I do? Do? DO?

No way out! No way out?

No air! No air? Where is the air? There is no air. There is only water. Water everywhere. Everywhere. Everywhere. I can feel the water. I am the water. It's my clothes, skin, body, hair, ears, eyes, face, mouth, nose.

Why did I stay?

Everyone else was right. I was wrong. How could I be so wrong?

Face. Mouth. Nose. Mouth.

It's going to take me.

Mouth. Nose. Mouth. Nose.

I can't brave this. I'm not strong enough. I can't get out. There is no way out.

Mouth. Nose. Throat. Throat.

The water is swirling, whirling, crashing, lashing, black.

Throat. Throat. Lungs. Lungs.

What can I do? Nothing. Nothing. Nothing.

Black.

Isabella Olivares
J. M. Tate High School
11th Grade, Karen MacDonald

What You TRULY Are...

Stop tricking me like that
You. Tell me this when you mean something
different
Creativity destroying my own free will
On the outside I do what you're asking
Psychopathic thoughts run through your head
Having such a toll on my mind
And even though you say I may know what's in
control
Neither of us knows that, that is
actually true
Thankfully, I'm smarter than you.

Emma Jowers
Fort Walton Beach High School
10th Grade, Amy Holt

Faith in Society

Human nature is a key part in how society acts and what society does. People do certain things and have specific views on a topic based on how others have shown themselves to be perceived. But what happens when one person's actions become a brand for a whole group of people? What happens when society gets a false perception on an assembly of people based on one bad experience? The world falls into a place full of hatred towards others. But what about when the world has hatred upon a group of people who have been called on to love others, a group of people who label themselves as different because of how they show their faith through kindness and courage.

Christianity is a religion based on the idea that love wins. We as a group have the belief that our God loved us enough to send down his one and only son to save us from a life of sin and show us extreme grace, mercy, and forgiveness. But many people today view us as hypocrites, how did this happen? The group of people whose biggest commandment was to "love your neighbor as yourself" have become known to be one of the most judgmental accumulation of individuals. Admittedly, there is a small community of Christians who discriminate against other people with different beliefs than them. But this small minority should not be labeled as the whole group itself. The younger generation of Christians are trying to relabel what we have begun to be perceived as. We are trying to rename this religion as what it was originally intended to be.

People today claim that Christianity is not true. That the resurrection never truly happened and that the whole thing is just a story people came up with to keep the movement alive. But history itself, proves that there was a man named Jesus Christ who performed miracles and did in fact die and rise from the dead. We don't believe in Jesus because the Bible tells us so, we believe in Jesus because the people tell us so. We know Jesus existed because stories have been passed down from person to person and texts have been written and there have been eye witness accounts of people who saw him die on a cross and rise back up again. If you look back at documents created, you can form a timeline showing how closely these events did happen and how they date back to being true.

Another one of the largest arguments against Christianity is, if God really does exist why is there pain and suffering in the world. Though this makes sense, people do not realize that making everything better is not what God does. The Lord takes our mistakes and shows us extreme mercy and forgiveness about it and showing himself through us and letting us be a beacon of light. Furthermore, if we believe God doesn't exist to make things good, then how come people of all faiths flee to the church in time of need? After the 9/11 terrorist attacks on the United States, church attendance flew through the roof. There was a spike in the amount of people who attended, and the diversity seen for two weeks after these attacks. Then rates dropped down to a normal level. (Who Needs God, Andy Stanley) People find peace in believing that there is a divine being who will help us in time of need, but only when that kind of protection is needed.

Though many people will try to argue against faith, they cannot help but wonder what it is about. People are naturally drawn to a light in the darkness, and what they don't realize is that this light is God. People who claim that Jesus doesn't exist spend more time trying to disprove the facts than exploring the idea that maybe something is out there. Everyone is entitled to their own beliefs and what they think is true, but sometimes you can't help but be curious about one man who created everything in the universe and knows it by name.

Jakeane Foster
J. M. Tate High School
11th Grade, Karen MacDonald

Soul Spirit

My soul an unspoken blessing,
it has the fire, it burns bright.
I am headstrong and I am light.
The blessings come and never go.
They follow me high and far below.
My soul is strong and I know why.
It teaches me things, and it helps me out.
I will not whisper, I will shout,
because this is what my soul is about.

Lacey Toyne
J. M. Tate High School
11th Grade, Karen MacDonald

Pernicious

People are evil
Everyone has a dark side
Revenge is a sweet, sweet victory
No one is vicious at birth
Instead it's what you learn
Can no longer sustain happy thoughts
Instead you became sour
Obvious pain haunts your brain
Unable to get away
Stay away from people who irk you.

Kendall Moreland

Fort Walton Beach High School
9th Grade, Amy Holt

A Series of Codes

We all know what it's like to feel unwanted and unworthy at times but Josh lives this everyday watching potential families pass the Buffalo room not even turning to look. He grew up in the nursery where all of the unwanted and less intelligent kids go. From the cracked window that just recently came into Josh's field of view, he stared and saw the receptionist in her neat uniform answering the calls of potential families. He grows up and longs to be on his own in the world.

Eventually, he reaches 18 and sets out on his own journey of life. He put himself through school, got a job, and other normal things someone of his age would do. Josh took pride in his role in the workplace and community. He's grown out of almost everything that made him the 100 point child or maybe he has just masked it, with his insurmountable success. He's finally collected enough Parent Points (PP) to do what he wants. Josh had always wanted a child of his own and wanted to give a child the life he never had when he was younger. He had quickly lost count of all the social workers who have politely hid their expressions of doubt when he said he wanted to adopt a 100 point child. Josh was willing to do whatever it takes to even get *one* parent point. The employees at the Child Services Center asked him about his upbringing and he just shrugged it off with a smile. He didn't exactly want to talk about his past as a man of his stature would be shunned for his childhood.

Finally, he's got the points, he's got the experience, and he's had to sit through the long, monotone professor's lectures. After all his training, yes, he was legally ready to adopt a child, but he wasn't mentally ready. All he had ever known was to fight for himself and never had to worry about anyone else. One decision and Josh's world will be flipped upside down, but he's thought long and hard about this. Plenty of sleepless nights and daydreaming has lead him to believe he is now ready to raise a child of his own.

The facility's staff welcomes him with open arms, eyes scanning his wrinkle free suit with hair freshly cut and a shiny, gold watch perched up on his wrist. "Right this way Mr. Wilson" the receptionist motions for him to follow her down the narrow, freshly painted hall. She's taking him to the higher point value children, which becomes evident when they pass a door and the sound of cries echo through the building. Before they get too much further, she runs Josh's stats and a 6 digit number pops up on the screen. She sends a delightful smile his way in regards to his staggering amount of points.

They arrive at a colorful room with brand new books and a wonderful teacher playing with the kids. Josh looks at the little plaque on the wall that reads *Butterfly Room; Advanced learning and communicating skills. 80,000-120,000 PP.* Josh cringes at the sight of this seemingly delightful place, nothing like the place he remembered. Josh was noticing the children's expressions, and they all seemed like they were having a great time and that they weren't forced to be there. He takes interest in these kids and suddenly Josh didn't want a child comparable to his own upbringing. He wanted a child of the most rich childhood but only because of something he saw in this nursery. Josh swore he saw a child move in a very erratic way and it seemed to happen multiple times in a short time period. Once the receptionist began to see this herself, she became very frantic and was pushing Josh to the next room, but he was stuck. Right in that moment, Josh knew that was the child he wanted and the lady couldn't, and wouldn't change his mind, considering her position relies on the amount of "sales." He gets home that night and began to deeply research the system and exactly how it works because children aren't supposed to glitch, and he was sure of that. Josh went through the whole process and eventually brought home the child he had spent every waking minute thinking about the seeming supernatural event that had occurred right in front of his eyes, and it wasn't on purpose. Josh had really made this child feel like he had a home and Josh fell in love with this child, but creating a family wasn't his plan. He asked her if she had any preferences on her name and said she had always liked *Lilly*. Josh agreed as he had a feeling she wouldn't be with him for long.

One night, Lilly was sleeping and Josh walked in her room, walls the color of cotton candy. She was shivering, so he pulled her comforter up to her neck. But under the blanket, he noticed a bright blue light coming from her wrist, so he investigated and it was coming from inside her skin and he woke her up. Lilly being the typical 7-year-old she was, sprung out of her bed and was ready to put together the kitten puzzle Josh had gotten her the night before. Josh stopped her before she got too much further and questioned her, and she was sent into panic mode. Lilly acted out in such a way that lead Josh to believe something was horribly wrong. She was very protective and immediately grabbed her arm and hid it in her shirt. She also became very aggressive and started to yell at Josh, and this just furthered his theory something just wasn't right. Josh brought her to their local hospital, and they too became very suspicious and sent him home without an explanation as of why this occurred. The next night Josh noticed the same thing happening and he decided to leave it be, he had grown to love Lilly as his daughter and couldn't stand the thought of her just being an experiment. But over the next few months Josh started to notice everybody has this glowing blue patch on their arm, except for him. He had brought it up to multiple people and they seemed to be concerned and Josh started to feel the same way for himself. He had made an appointment with the town's only therapist as soon as they could see him. Josh arrived to his appointment 15 minutes early as he was instructed by the lady that he conversed with on the phone. The paperwork was done and he was sent back into the dim and dingy room with a brown bed and blank white walls that seemed to stare back at him. Josh explained everything that had been happening and she prescribed him with a medication that he was to take every day and never skip a day, or he would be terribly sorry. Josh wasn't one to rebel against the doctor and he did exactly as she said, these "visions" of his seemed to slowly disappear until they were completely gone.

Life at the Wilson's house had gotten as normal as it could. The family of two started to fall into routine and they were both happy as could be with their new lifestyle. Lilly had later on informed Josh she had never been on a vacation of any sort. Times for Josh at work had made this a perfect time to go and Lilly had excelled in her second grade class at the *Magnolia Private School for the Gifted.*

Josh and Lilly both packed for their lavish vacation to the Fiji Islands. Upon arrival to their private hotel room on the cliff side of a mountain, Josh's phone buzzed reminding him to take his medication he had made sure to refill before their trip. Searching both bags, he realized he had left the bottle on the counter at home and there was no way he was going to get that prescription filled here. Josh skipped his medication for 6 days and those "visions" had starting to come back, for each day he was without it, the hallucinations grew stronger. On the seventh and final day of the vacation, Josh seemed to have left reality and gone into a desert-like place and a sort of announcement echoed through this place.

It explained that Josh had entered what was left of humanity and the planet. He was a part of the few people that were left on the Earth, nothing he ever saw had been real, but it was a sort of programmed lifestyle were everything he saw or did or even the people he met were just space fillers to create a life around Josh. All controlled by a computer. Josh was the only person that could see the blue lights and the simulated therapist gave him a medication that wasn't real, it was just so that when the programmers changed the wiring of his brain, the effects would seem normal. The higher power that controlled life as he knew it, missed something in Josh's brain when he was assessed as a baby and he wasn't supposed to be able to see those lights. Everything started to come together, he had heard an Old Wives Tales about "The world being completely wiped out" but never thought anything of it. Josh's life has all been a lie ever since he was born, he really wasn't in control as he thought he was. Josh had also come to the conclusion of what made him a child of lesser value, he was the only real child at that nursery and all the other kids were more intelligent because the programmers had made them just that, perfect. As for the other 100 point children, they were real too, but finding and explaining the situation now would be virtually impossible. He isn't even a part of the human race, everything he's ever known has been but a series of codes.

Chase Tolbert
J. M. Tate High School
11th Grade, Karen MacDonald

All These Trophies Watching Me

I am silent trophy
Sitting on the dresser
Watching
Judging
Silence…
But I can see you
Slithering through the rules
Making the curveball unworthy

Kyndal Milsted
J. M. Tate High School
11th Grade, Karen MacDonald

Silent Thunderstorm

My heart is a silent thunderstorm
Quiet lightning striking my heart
Thunder rumbling
Blood pumping rapidly when I hear the wind
Then suddenly the beats stop with the rain

Kaitlyn Kincaid
Fort Walton Beach High School
10th Grade, Amy Holt

Hanahaki Disease

花吐き病

~Prologue~

*"**Hanahaki Disease** is a disease in which the victim coughs up flower petals when they suffer from one-sided love. It ends when the beloved returns their feelings (romantic love only; a strong friendship is not enough), or when the victim dies. It can be cured through surgical removal, but when the infection is removed, the victim's romantic feelings for their love also disappear."* (fanlore.org/wiki/Hanahaki_Disease)

$$/\ /\ \_\ -\ \_\ -\ \_\ /\ /\ \_\ -\ \_\ -\ \_\ /\ /$$

Adonia Castellanos is a 17-year-old girl with an illness that will kill her if she isn't cured soon. She has been suffering from this disease for half of a year now, she only has 6 months left before she dies. She refuses to get the surgical procedure done because she believes that he will love her. She knows it deep down in her heart.

You see, she's fallen in love with a boy named Maxwell Brown. But sadly, he doesn't love her back, hell he doesn't even know that she exists. They were best friends back in elementary and middle school. Once high school started they went their separate ways, she had a hard time with the split.

Adonia did everything in her power to keep their bond, but Maxwell moved on quickly, leaving her in the dust. She loved him, and still does, it pains her to see him with everyone but her. She fears that he hates her.

$$/ / \_ - \_ - \_ / / \_ - \_ - \_ / /$$

Maxwell Brown, an 18-year-old boy, afraid of love. He left his childhood best friend because he was afraid of hurting her. He was in love with her...

The last thing he wanted to do was break her heart, but little did he know that he had done just that. He hasn't talked to her in 4 years. Poor Adonia, he feels horrible for leaving her so quickly and without telling her his reasoning. He sees her in the halls frequently and what he has noticed is that she doesn't walk with anyone to her classes.

And at lunch, she doesn't sit with anyone. She's always alone when he sees her. He thought that she would be able to make at least one friend by her senior year. He feels so much remorse for leaving her all alone.

/ / _ - _ - _ / / _ - _ - _ / /

~Chapter 1~

Adonia clicks her pen as she watches the hands on the clock tick by, she's more than ready to go home. The pain in her chest is becoming too much to bear. She can feel the petals rising from her lungs like a fire screaming to be let out. The bell rings, she dashes out of the classroom and hurries to the bathroom.

As she throws the petals up, she begins to wish that she never fell in love. She's so stupid to make such a mistake. She promised herself that she'd never fall for him. She's been trying to distract herself from him.

She exits the bathroom after cleaning herself up. She hates herself more and more every day.

"Why do I deal with this crap? Why can't I just stop loving him?? He's just a dumb boy... just a dumb boy..." she mutters to herself, tears welling up in her eyes when the last words escape her mouth. She inhales deeply, trying her best not to cry. She strides out of the school, to meet up with her mom. She climbs into the car.

"Honey, you really need to reconsider the procedure... you only get weaker day by day. Your father and I are really worried about you." Mrs. Castellanos' voice is full of concern for her daughter's health.

"I know mom..." Adonia's voice trails off. Maxwell walks by the car with a girl, he smiles at her, it looks genuine. Adonia shoots them a pained look when they aren't watching. She burst out in tears, "It's not fair mom! He just left me with no warning or anything!" she sobs. Her mom reaches over the center console and hugs her.

"I'm sorry baby, it's gonna be okay. Just remember: boys are dumb." Adonia's mom says softly. On the ride home, Adonia's mom took her to her favorite restaurant. In an attempt to cheer her up.

~Chapter 2~

Maxwell saw Adonia as he was walking with his friend. She was in so much pain and he could tell, just by a quick glance at her eyes, they held so much sadness. He knew that he was to blame for it.

"Maxie are you okay?" the girl next him looked at him with concern. Her voice was squeaky and she had long brown hair that ran down her back and brushed her hips, and sunkissed skin with tons of freckles, she was quite thin but in a fit sense.

"Yeah, I'm fine. Thanks, Daphne." Maxwell sighed and smiled at her.

"Okayyy. Soooo, are you doing anything this afternoon?" Daphne smiled, showing her dimples.

"No, I'm not doing anything. I think...I'm just going to go home and do my schoolwork." Maxwell's eyes are covered with a guilty glass.

"D-do you mind if I stop by for a few hours to study with you?" her cheeks were a light pink.

"Um...no I don't mind." Maxwell gives her a side smile.

"Okay! Great! That's awesome! Alright cool! I'll see you at 2:30 then." Daphne skips off.

"...yep..." he sighs.

~Chapter 3~

The winter formal is coming up and everyone is running around asking each other to the dance with fancy signs and routines. Lunchtime comes around and today Maxwell decides to sit with a certain messy haired, silver-eyed, petite girl named Adonia. She doesn't notice him at first, not until he clears his throat. Her eyes dart up from her book and instantly fill with tears.

"M-max?" she stammers.

"Yeah, Adonia...I'm really sorry..." he furrows his eyebrows and remorse fills his expression.

"It's whatever..." Adonia looks down as she holds back an ocean from slipping out.

"Adonia, I know what I did wasn't right." Maxwell holds her chin and gently tips her head up so she is looking at him, "I'm sorry. I left because-"

"Can we not do this in public? Please. I'd love to chat on this subject...just not here. Please." her voice begins to break.

"Uh...yeah. Anything for you." Maxwell smiles softly at her.

"Meet at the park after school? On the jungle gym?" Adonia returns the smile.

"Yeah. Sounds great." he looks at her with sad eyes.

"Okay, great." Adonia returns to reading her book.

~Chapter 4~

After school Adonia awaits Maxwell's arrival on top of the jungle gym. Maxwell runs to the park, eager to not let her down...again. He trips stumbles onto the jungle gym, finally making it.

"You're 30 minutes late." Adonia sits on the slide, facing away from him.

"I'm sorry but the high school isn't as close as the middle school was." he breathes heavily, trying to catch his breath.

"Okay...so...um why did you abandon me?" Adonia's voice is full of sorrow and ferocity.

"Because I love you! I was afraid of you not returning the feelings and then I'd get sick, and then the only way for my survival would be to get it surgically removed and then I would feel *nothing* towards you. And that's the last thing I want. I want to be with you Adonia. I'm so sorry that I left you. I'm so sorry." Maxwell bursts into tears, sobs rip from his chest.

"Max…" Adonia feels a burning sensation in her chest, the fire rises and then disappears completely, "I love you too. I always have, and I'm afraid that I always will." tears slip down her cheeks. *'It's finally over…'* she thinks. She turns around and hugs Maxwell tightly. He returns the tight embrace with one of his own.

"I'm so sorry Adonia. I should've never left you alone…" he sniffles.

"It's alright, I promise." She smiles truly, it's been a long time since she's smiled genuinely.

~End~

Angelina McCormick
Max Bruner Jr. Middle School
7th Grade, Katrina Brownsberger

The Pool Incident

Hey, I'm Daniel, and this is the story of how I overcame my first and only, childhood bully. It was just a normal day, I got up, ate breakfast, and went to the bus stop. I saw my friend Thomas on the bus and we talked the whole way to school about normal 14-year-old boy stuff, like who would win in a fight: robot chickens, or an angry cat (I said robot chickens, he said angry cat). When we finally got to school, I didn't want to go inside. I knew that Jeremy was going to be there, waiting for me. Jeremy is my bully, he's that annoyingly popular guy at school that you hate, but deep down inside, you kind of want to be friends with them, and you hate that part of you, but it's always kind of there. He's got slicked back blonde dyed hair and wears the most expensive clothes because apparently, that's "cool". About a month ago, Jeremy found out a secret about me and spread the rumor throughout the school, that I'm gay. Since he's "the popular guy", the rumor spread like wildfire, and before you knew it, everyone knew I was gay. People would see me in the halls and say something entirely rude (I'd rather not say what). I was

43

starting to get tired of all these dumb bullies, but of course I could never say anything, because that would just make it worse. So, when I walked into school, not to my surprise, Jeremy was standing there, waiting to yell something terrible at me (None of the teachers or adults know anything about this situation). Before Jeremy could say anything, I ran past him straight to my locker, and then to my homeroom. We share the same 4th, 5th, and 6th period, so my first three classes weren't so bad. Even though Jeremy was still being a huge jerk, everyone else had gotten over the rumor a while ago. When the bell had eventually rang for 4th period, the anxiety started rushing through me, like a dam had just broke and the river started flowing. I felt like I was going to collapse. I got to the door, and stepped in the classroom and looked around, expecting to see Jeremy, but I didn't. I wondered "Was he late?" "Did he get picked up?" I was sorely mistaken. Little did I know, that he was standing right behind me, like a predator about to pounce on its prey, then it happened, he pounced. Jeremy scared me half to death and I almost peed my pants, and I shrieked so loud your eardrums could've burst. While I was crying my eyes out from the horror, Jeremy and everyone else was just snickering at me and my scaredness. I felt like I was about to have a panic attack, but before I could ask, the teacher excused me to the bathroom to get myself together. As I was leaving the room, I could still hear laughter behind me and then the teacher telling the class to settle down. When I finally got to the bathroom after what felt like forever, I felt like I was going to throw up, and then I did… I got back to the classroom in time to head to the lunchroom, but after what had happened, I wasn't in the mood to eat. Luckily, Thomas was in the class with me, so he made me feel better during lunch. When lunch was over, we got back to class and the teacher told us a few announcements before we started class. He told us that we would be having a field trip to a public pool next week, and Thomas and I were ecstatic. He said the field trip was to be a relaxing trip to clear our minds for the big test we'd have the day after, but since it was science class, we also would be having to do something "sciencey". The class decided to do a project on how much chlorine was in the pool. Anyways, we all knew that it was going to be a pretty cool field trip, and the whole class was super excited. Especially because the teacher, whose name was Mr. Laceman, was actually a pretty cool, fun, and laid back guy. Mr. Laceman was my favorite teacher, and probably always will be. Mr. Laceman is proudly gay, but no one ever thought anything bad of it, which is why I was so puzzled as to why I was bullied so much. Everyone in the class was very excited for the field trip we'd be having the next week, even me! Even though Jeremy would be there, I would still have time to clear my mind from everything and study for the test. I was foolishly wrong to think that everything would be fine though, because I had no idea that this field trip would probably end up being the worst day in my pathetic little life. A week later, I get up one morning for school and look at the calendar on my wall and realize it, "Today's the day!" I exclaimed. I was exponentially excited, I got out of bed, got all my school stuff together, and ran to the bus stop, I didn't even eat breakfast, that's how excited I was. The bus finally came and picked me up and of course I sat by Thomas. We were talking about how awesome the pool was going to be and how we couldn't wait. We completely forgot about Jeremy because we were so excited, but we didn't even care. When we got to school, and our homeroom classes, the loudspeaker turned on, "If you are attending the science field trip to the public pool, please report to the gymnasium." it said, and so I did. When I got to the gym, I immediately shot Thomas a look so we could pair up and sit together on the bus. Once the teachers took role, everyone got on the bus, and we drove off. It was a 30 minute drive to the public pool, so for the first 10 minutes of the bus ride, Mr. Laceman went through the procedures we'd take once we arrived, like when we got there, wait for them to let us off the bus and other basic stuff. After his lecture was over, we were allowed to talk as we wished, so of course Thomas and I blabbered the whole way there. We had finally gotten to the pool and we were let off the bus into the shower room to put on our bathing suits. They counted us again and after they made sure everyone was there, we were let into the pool. It was a really nice, beautiful pool, and the water was crystal clear. There were huge awesome water slides and diving boards towering over the pool. There weren't many other people there, so we basically got the whole pool to ourselves. The trip was pretty fun, getting to mess around in the water and swim around with Thomas. The science project of seeing how much chlorine was in the pool was really easy too, all we had to do was ask the pool keeper, it was 64%. Anyways, after we were done with that, Jeremy came up to me with a dumb dare. He wanted me to jump off of the 20 ft high diving board. I said no for what felt like an eternity until he finally gave up and said he would do it himself. He got to the top of the diving board and before you could do or say anything, he yelled "Daniel, your so gay!" in a mocking tone, and then he cannonballed into the water and splashed everyone. I was so angry and I decided, I'd had finally had enough of him, so I jumped into the water, I went over to him, and without a second thought, I sucker-punched him right in the face. His nose started bleeding, but I hadn't had enough of him yet, so I kept on going. He started fighting back and before long, this had been turned into an ugly fist fight in a public pool. One of the kids went and got Mr. Laceman who hadn't seen any of this and told him everything that had just happened. Mr. Laceman had to get up and with another kid had to pull Jeremy and me off of each other because we knew we couldn't stop fighting until there was a clear winner. Mr. Laceman then pulled us aside away from the pool and asked us what was going on and what just happened between us. Of course, as to not get in trouble, Jeremy lied and said it was nothing but a "misunderstanding" and "it won't happen again". I rolled my eyes so hard at the statement they might as well have rolled back in my head, but Mr. Laceman didn't notice, then he asked me what it was all about. I didn't want to get in trouble or get Jeremy mad at me so I just agreed with him. Mr. Laceman looked at us as if he knew something, and then he let Jeremy go. Once Jeremy left, he asked me again, then the floodgates opened and I spilled out everything that had been happening the past month and that day. He seemed almost not surprised, like he knew. It concerned me a little, and then he sighed and told me he understood. Apparently, he had had the same thing happen to him before when he was in 8th grade. I was surprised, because he seemed like such a cool guy I would've never guessed this had ever happened to him. He told me that ignoring it is ok, but it's better to tell an adult so they could help you, he also told me that I am no different, and that I don't have to be ashamed of what anyone -Jeremy- says. This whole fiasco of a field trip became known as "the pool incident" from then on. The next day when I came to school, I was ready for the test and more confident than ever! When I walked into the school though, I didn't see Jeremy anywhere. I just assumed that he had finally given up due to what happened the day prior. I in fact didn't see him in the halls either, which was good and concerning at the same time. As the bell for 4th period rang, I headed to the classroom half expecting to see Jeremy there, and he was sitting right there, in his desk. I was a little confused, but I didn't think anything of it, until Thomas told me that he heard that Jeremy was in the principal's office this morning! I immediately felt really bad! Just because I didn't want to be bullied by him, that didn't mean I wanted him to get in trouble! What had I done?! After class was over though, Jeremy did the completely unexpected, he came up to me, and apologized! What he said next, well, it was really unexpected, he whispered in my ear, "I'm just like you, I'm gay." My heart was racing, "Why is he telling me this, what is happening?!", I thought. He kept talking while I was completely stunned, "Look okay, I'm honestly really sorry and I know this might be a little weird but, I've been bullying you because I like you, and I was ashamed but I really do…" I didn't know what to say, then what he did next caught me so off guard that I almost flinched, he leaned in for a hug and said, "Can we please just start over?" I didn't know what to say other than yes, just to be nice. I don't regret a thing I did or said that day, because fast forward a year and here I am, dating Jeremy, happy and together. And anytime someone brings up "the pool incident", Jeremy and I just laugh it off and say it was "nothing".

Savannah Beaulieu
Fort Walton High School
10th Grade, Lynne Shirley

Sowing Sword-Lilies

Iridescent streaks across your reflection,
Liquid pooling around your sneakers even in the
heat.
Your skin burns as the sun pounds
From the blazing blue sky above
Sweat drips from your hair and soaks your neck;
Storm-clouds gather in the distance,
Promising shelter.

Someday, you want to plant a garden,
Nurture it to growth;
Watch fresh green crumble the tar,
Returning it to earth,
Watch the bulbs of the sword-lilies spread wide
Dance among the flowers and feel yourself bloom
with them,
Put your roots down and reach for the sun.

Zoë Deer
Fort Walton Beach High School
9th Grade, Amy Holt

Underwater

Underwater, where light is dimmed
And fish swim oblivious to the danger below
Underwater, where the currents are always being
changed
And sea creatures use them as transportation

Where sharks swim in groups
And danger lurks in the darkest depths
Where light no longer reaches
Lurks mythological and undiscovered creatures
That lay near vents of hearth

Underwater, where ancient cities hide
And history fades away
Underwater, where ships have died
And many lives perished with them

Underwater, where our thoughts are clouded
And we drown in sadness
Underwater, where our will swims away
And we let go

Underwater, where light is dimmed
And fish swim oblivious to the danger below

Underwater, where the currents are always being
changed
And sea creatures use them as transportation

Quinterra Nichols
Fort Walton Beach High School
11th Grade, Amy Holt

When I Dance. . .

I have never spoken so clearly until the day my
feet hit the floor.
My tongue tied shut but my body, an open mouth
telling you my story as the music flows through
my veins.
Notes leading my body to say the things I could
never utter.
When I dance,
the world becomes a library; I am an open book.
My soul, a tale I am sharing.
Have you noticed when I dance I am speaking?
These sharp movements turned to shouts. My feet
carrying the spirit of my voice.
I don't think, I just move.
Every leap, every turn, every breath is me giving
all.
The twirl of my hands pouring out secrets you'll
probably never catch. And I emerge from the
shadows I am always hiding in.
When I dance,
the expressions on my face become pages of
chapters I have yet to write. The music, a pen I
lead with my heart.
Can you read between the lines?

When I dance, there is no doubt. There is no fear.
For once, I don't question who I am, why I am or
if I should change.
I love myself because of the music within me. It is
embroidered into the edges of my soul.
Stitches weaving in and out every time I move,
transforming into a fabric I am falling so deeply
in love with that I try to enclose my body into it
whenever I get the chance.
When I dance, I forget.
I forget about my worries, my struggles and my
insecurities.
Sometimes I even forget where I am, but that's
okay because usually I am in a place I don't want
to be.
Except now, when I'm entrapped in this music.
Writing words never said, telling stories that have
never left my tongue.
Can you hear them?

Joseph Zylak
Fort Walton Beach High School
10th Grade, Amy Holt

Half-Breed

I was a freak. This was a label that I had been given from the day I was born. Ever since my drunkard of a father had the misfortune of being left with me, I was reminded of my title on the daily. I was, by the nature of my birth, an oddity that most saw as unnatural. My mother's caravan had traveled into town many years ago and my father made it his goal to get with the woman who had the fairest hair and greenest eyes; at least for a night. This night brought along a consequence that he did not expect. It brought me, his half-breed of a son.

The townsfolk of my home knew my family well. I heard every last bit of gossip said by both my peers and their parents; it was always horrendous words that would leave their lips. I recall hearing them say, "I've always heard that Elves grant wishes. I wonder if Jacob's boy can do that," or, "Don't look into that kid's eyes! He might curse you or somethin'," or even, "If that kid ever dies, cut his ears off. I hear they're good luck." It was repulsive, the way they acted towards me. I knew for a fact that if I were truly one of their own, I would never receive even half the disrespect they gave me; if I was born a man with normal ears, dark eyes, and was built like a brute, then and only then could the people of my home see me as an equal. But instead, I had to be born different. I had to be tall and slender; my eyes had to be a shiny emerald green; my ears had to be long, narrow, and pointed sharply at the end. My own neighbors embedded the fact that I was a mistake into every fiber of my being. It was because of this, that I ventured North. I could no longer tolerate the constant berating. I didn't want to accept that I was, an abomination of nature. I needed to find my mother, the one who left me alone in the first place.

Admittedly, I knew it would be difficult for me to find a good ride to the North. Considering that the only person in my town who owned cart horses wanted my ears, I couldn't exactly ask him for help. Most men didn't want to travel into Elvish territory anyway, mostly out of the fear that they may be shot with an arrow upon sight. There always seemed to be a bit of *mild* hostility from both races when they were in the same room. Most of the time neither were bold enough to speak with one another; and the ones that were usually ended up fighting with each other. My mother was a different story, or so I've been told. The couple in charge of the library told me things when I went there to read; they were the only true kind folk that resided in my home. My mother moved around in a caravan made of dark brown wood that had intricate carvings all over it. She was a traveling artisan, selling her creations to any who would buy them. Crafting was a common profession amongst Elves, but speaking and trading with men was not nearly as ordinary. She met my father in the tavern and, I believe due to drinking too much, stayed with him for the night. She then proceeded to stay with him until I was born. Soon afterwards, she left in the middle of the night, not saying a word to anyone.

~~~~~~~~~

The snow was something I had read about many times, but never seen in person. I found myself taking mental notes while I walked through the woods. When snow fell down from the sky it settled into thick masses on the trees. When the mass of the snow was too much, it fell down into a lonely pile upon the ground. Snow, like most things, was fickle. It was either falling from the sky, falling from a tree, or melting to start falling all over again. It was like snow was always on the run from something. I was not fond of it. I learned quickly that I was not fond of most things the North offered me. From my perspective, all aspects of the North were frustrating. The way that I had to struggle to walk along the snowy pathway. The fact that the air was so cold that it hurt to breathe in. The constant fear that my journey here was pointless; that I'd never reach my goal of seeing my mother.

After a long time trudging along the path, I eventually reached a rather large clearing in the forest. In the center of it was an utterly massive tree, a kind that had never been upon my eyes before. It had a very thick trunk and had grown up very high above its neighbors. The leaves of the tree were all intact, and they seemed to faintly shimmer like silver when light was hitting them. A large building had been constructed in it, a tree fort of sorts. Although, it was by far something much more impressive than other tree forts I had seen. The windows were lit up, and I could see figures moving around inside. There was a wooden ladder that seemed to lead up to the inside. Not far from the base of the tree, I saw a few caravans, each with a unique look to it. I took in a deep breath and approached.

There were five caravans in total. They were all similar in size, but were each made using different woods and decorations. From what I had heard, things of Elvish construction were all very unique. I ran my hand along the one closest to me. It was as if I could feel all the time and effort, the love that it took to make it. I blinked, beginning to further analyze the vehicle I was touching. It was constructed using a dark brown wood, most likely from a tree in this area. I stared at the different symbols and markings covering it, feeling a lump in my throat. None of the people who owned these caravans were inside of them or outside. My eyes turned to the large tree.

~~~~~~~~~~

Climbing up the creaky wooden ladder, I pushed open the old hatch and lifted myself inside, closing the hatch behind me. In front of me now was a wooden door; above it was a rectangular sign that had Elvish script inscribed into it. Despite wanting to be proficient at it, I never got the chance to learn much Elvish; there was only one small book that I managed to buy off a trader that came into town. I was able to roughly translate the sign as: "Compassion". It seemed to be a bit of an odd name for whatever this place was, but it was inviting at the very least. I quietly opened the door, soundlessly closing it as I slinked inside of the main room. The people inside didn't seem to notice me. I knew where I was as soon as I saw the scenery: There were a few different tables around, each with four chairs. In each chair sat a different individual; the traits that linked them being their pointed ears and glasses of drink. There were a number of different decorations adorning the walls:

small paintings, little trinkets on shelves, and some banners that had intricate designs on them. I knew from the evidence that I was inside of a tavern; my father had introduced me to them long ago.

I took in a deep breath, beginning to approach the bar. While I took my small steps, I began to feel something in my chest. This was perplexing. I was *here*, I was at my destination. Why was it now that I felt nervous? I could understand the fear I had before reaching the tree tavern; I thought I would never even come close to the land of Elves. Now that I was here though, there was a feeling in my chest that I had never felt before. I had assumed that it was anxiety or fear, but was it really? It felt as though there was an endless pit within my stomach, as if my very chest was a sinkhole collapsing in upon itself. Within my throat was a pressure, a pain, a sensation that should have made me scared; it was the sort of feeling that one would experience when they are surrounded by a group of rogues armed with daggers. Despite this, I wasn't running away as I would if confronted by thugs of that nature. I realized what I was feeling as I sat down on a barstool. It was excitement, genuine excitement.

Once I was seated, the barkeep behind the counter approached me and asked a question in his native tongue. I quickly responded with, "I'm quite sorry, but I don't exactly speak Elvish very well." He simply smiled at me.

"No worries friend. All are welcome here in my tree, whether you can say anything or not. What can I get you to drink?" he said, chuckling softly. He spoke in a very joyful, friendly manner, something that brought a smile to my own face.

"I'll just have some water, thank you," I replied, still smiling. His more laid-back attitude started to radiate off of him and onto me. "Do you get many mute people in here?" I asked as he poured me my cup of water.

"Not recently, but if someone mute did come in I'd serve him just the same. He might have to write down what he wants, but he'd get it!" the barkeep answered, laughing as he passed me my cup. He was so much more jovial than any other individual I had interacted with in the past. It was like he didn't even notice that I looked different to him. "So, if you don't mind me asking, what brings you to my tree, friend?" the barkeep asked casually.

"I'm looking for someone. My mother. I believe I saw her caravan outside. She left me down in the South with my father soon after I was born," I answered, staring at the now wide-eyed Elf in front of me.

"You're Rahasia's son?" he asked in a loud, surprised tone. This caught the attention of a table close to the bar. The table had three patrons seated at it, each wearing a purple hooded cloak. I watched as one of them lifted off her hood, revealing long fair hair, striking green eyes, and ears that pointed out sharply.

~~~~~~~~~

I stared at my mother's face for a bit as we sat across from each other. Her slender features, eye color, and ear shape were identical to mine. There was no denying her status as my mother. I continued to observe her appearance, leaving pure silence between the two of us. She eventually grew tired of the silence, slowly saying "I suppose you have some questions for me." She spoke in a gentle manner, her voice a bit on the higher side. I took in a deep breath and gingerly released it. I expected myself to be mad, or at the very least still excited to talk with her for the first time. Instead, I could feel tears welling up in my eyes. "Why did you leave me alone with *them*?" I asked, trying my best to not cry in front of her. I could feel the same pressure in my throat that I felt earlier. I stared into my mother's eyes, seeing very little emotion in them. Poems had always described the eyes of Elves to be bright and gleaming, and while those words could describe the eyes of who was before me now, that was all they were. They were almost sparkling with how green they were, a beautiful sight to behold. Yet, I saw within them no emotion, no remorse, no feelings of sorrow about the atrocity she had committed upon me. "You left me in the *comforting arms* of men who lack any form of kindness. How could you leave me, your *newborn* son, without a mother?" I could feel the tears streaming down my face now; whatever control I had over my body was gone now. My mother blinked and stared right back at me, replying to my misery with, "I did what I believed was best."

"I was in the back of the caravan with Vadania, carving wooden animals with her; most children in towns we visit beg their parents for those little toys. Aramil was driving the caravan down to the South. We hadn't been there yet; all we did know was that, as a whole, it was an area dominated by men. The town you were born in, as you surely know, has a yearly harvest festival that involves an awful lot of drinking. Aramil figured that we would be able to sell most of our things to the drunken townsfolk and make a large profit. We arrived, put our hoods up, and got to business. Seeing as I am fond of drinking as well, we took a break and went to the local Tavern. Vadania and Aramil only drank water; neither of them found it particularly fun to get intoxicated. I was seated at the bar, drinking with my cut of the coin we had made a few hours prior. Most of the patrons were so drunk they couldn't even tell that we were Elves. That was when I met your father. Due to the influence my many drinks had on me, I fell in love with him in that single evening. Despite my friends trying desperately to get me back to the caravan, I ignored them and went home with your father. They waited in the caravan for a week while I stayed with that man. Every day they would try and convince me that staying here was a terrible idea. I can be rather stubborn, especially when my mind is set upon something. As such, I adamantly refused every time. They eventually left me there. That was when I began to realize what I had done was not the best for *me*.

"When not inebriated and celebrating, the men of that town were not very kind to strangers that strolled into town; especially if they were Elvish. Your father tried his very best to keep me safe from the hateful locals. Even though he gave it his all, it wasn't enough to prevent my neighbors from disrespecting me on a daily basis. Things only got worse after you were born, which is why I chose to leave. I had received a letter from Vadania, asking me how I was and if my relationship was still as spectacular as I made it out to be. They were only a few towns over and would be coming by to say hello to me in person.

When they arrived I left with them, leaving whatever *life* I had made for myself in the South." My mother finished her story, the same emotionless look remaining in her eyes.

"You left me all alone because you had to deal with hostility?" I clenched my hand into a fist as I stared into her eyes, still crying as I asked the question. Nothing; I still saw nothing. "You are not very familiar with Elvish customs. This doesn't surprise me very much; many towns in the South don't educate children about other cultures very well, if at all. Elves, by our nature, can seem very self-centered from the perspectives of men. This self-centered mentality is a method of self-preservation, a way of keeping ourselves safe before anybody else. A common belief in Elvish culture is: if you're unable to properly take care of yourself, make yourself safe and happy, then you're in no condition to make others safe and happy. I left that town because a decision I had made put me in a situation where I endured constant stress and fear. I did what I was able to do in order to make myself safe. I began to prioritize myself over others." My mother looked back into my eyes as she spoke. I could tell she was seeing the conflicting emotions in my eyes: exasperation, sorrow, abandonment, loneliness. "Elves are not devoid of feelings, we just control them. That is the key cultural aspect that divides us and men. I've learned in my years since then to always keep myself in check, to think about things from a logical perspective. " She finished in a calm tone.

I asked myself which half of my blood I should define myself with; keeping emotions in check is an effective way of maintaining peace between people, but without emotions what drives you to do things? It was, after all, my own fears and worries that brought me to my mother in the first place. Abandoning logic all together isn't beneficial either; that can lead to hatred of others without justification. "I grew up surrounded by the views of men, I've seen the negative side of emotion. But I cannot simply accept logic. Your use of logic showed me the harm it can do unto others. I can't see the world separated in such black and white terms. There must be a better alternative," I stood up from the bar and looked at her, "the combination of logic and emotion will be what brings people together, regardless of race." As I finished speaking, I quickly exited the tree tavern. I walked back to the path, gently letting a sigh escape my lips. I looked around the clearing as I took my final steps away from the tree. It had stopped snowing.

Jalena Jarvis
Fort Walton Beach High School
9th Grade, Amy Holt

Epiphany

I'm the one I should love
I shouldn't need you
Your approval
Your anything.

I'm the one I should love
But I never did
Or have
Because of you.

I'm the one I should love
But because of you,
I had the idea
That you're the only one I should love.

I'm the one I should love
But I don't.
I've loved you for too long
But you never showed me love.

I'm the one I should love
But how can I,
When no one ever taught me,
Or showed me love?

I'm the one I should love
I always told you,
"I love you"
But you never once said those three words back.

I'm the one I should love
Over time,
I had realized
where I went wrong.

I shouldn't love you
Or cherish you
It should've been me...
It should've always been me...

Jaden Carlisle
Fort Walton Beach High School
9th Grade, Amy Holt

Flatline

Flatline
The sound of grief and despair
The sound that just isn't fair
The good ones hear it too soon
As they rise beyond the moon
Old souls go to lay
For they won't see another day
Flatline
The sound hospitals don't want to hear
Because their patients' end is growing near
Flatines
The sounds ears want to reject
Because they know how bad we feel wrecked
Families being torn apart
Death ripping out their hearts
Flatlines
We've all seen them, in our eyes or our minds
But that sound won't tear apart our binds
The binds of the deceased and loved
Flying high like doves
Soaring across the heavenly skies
As the tears flow from our eyes
Flatlines
When we hear those sounds running through our heads
We never forget the sound of the dead.

Jada Bard

Fort Walton Beach High School
10th Grade, Amy Holt

The Spectral Beast

Aloe Verra should have listened to him. He always told her time after time again to stay away from the small beast. To keep it in its cage and NEVER let it out. But, she didn't listen.

Aloe had heard its whimpering and terrible cries before and wished it to stop. She hated seeing animals in pain, so she would sneak scraps of food to it every chance she had, but it only phased through the creature's transparent body. It was already dead -she knew that- but that hadn't stopped its cries of pain. The poor thing was stitched together like some freaky Frankenstein badger-fox thing, only it wasn't even an animal anymore. Tick Tock called it "The Specter" and warned Aloe Verra to stay away from it and to leave it alone. For a four armed poofy-haired monster, TT could be scary when serious. But Aloe wasn't care. She didn't want The Specter to suffer anymore. So she waited until her foster mother, Ms. Daisy, and her monsterous mentor left the house.

When her home was finally silent Aloe rushed to the basement where the creature's cage lied. The

Specter lazily looked up from its napping spot and yawned, exposing its rows of rotting teeth. As Aloe quietly, quietly unlocked the cage door, the small beast hastily limped toward the silver bars, wagging its ghostly stubby tail. The hinges squeaked loudly as the cage door swung open freeing the poor creature. Its pale glowing eyes looked up at her almost in disbelief.

Then a smirk flashes across its face.

Giovanni De Lanoy
Fort Walton Beach High School
10th Grade, Amy Holt

The Memories of Victor W.

Prologue

I used to know.

I used to know many things. I still know many things. I have forgotten many things. I have forgotten much of my own personality. I know that I am adept in most scientific fields, as well as engineering; and I know that a machine of my own creation is the reason for my amnesia, as well as my being in this incredibly strange place. The only reason for my awareness of this machine is that of my first set of memories; which are the activation of said machine, followed by my waking up in this baffling world of yours. No, there is nothing between the two memories.

My journey, the story of my survival, is one I wish to tell at least once. I hope you don't mind my recounting it to you; however, I shall be speaking of it either way.

My troubles began when I woke up, finding myself lying in the soft grass of the forest.

Chapter 1

Yes, the ground was covered in soft, dark teal grass; which brushed against my hands as I rose from the cushion of the soil. Indescribably odd flora surrounded me on all sides; the confusing plant life was accompanied by oak trees with violet leaves. Needless to say, I was quite disturbed by the odd colors and unidentifiable foliage. However, I was disturbed even more by the fact that I had no memory of any experience with a regular tree so as to prove that the leaves were not supposed to be purple; I only had a gut feeling that it was wrong.

As I rose from the ground, neglecting the fact that the backs of my pants had been dirtied with soil and grass, I began to search my pockets. I felt this urge to identify myself, to figure out who I was; and the quickest way to do that was to find some form of identification. So, I searched my person high and low. In my breast pocket I found a note that read as such:

"Your name is Victor Wiggin, and you are a scientist. Your most recent project has been on hopping into alternate dimensions. The study has mostly been in quantum mechanics and particle physics; alongside the usual engineering that takes place in most of your projects. You do realize that there may be side effects in travelling to alternate realities, but the scientific discovery is worth the risk."

That is where the note hit its end. I folded the tattered paper once more, and returned it to my pocket. I continued scouring my person, finding a yellow pencil with a sharp, leaden tip in my right jacket pocket. In the left pocket of my coat was a small notebook bound in cherry red leather; the cover had the characters V.W. printed in gold lettering, which shimmered in the sunlight that managed to slip through the violet canopy up above. In my left pant pocket I found a photo of a man and a woman. I could only assume that the face of the man in the photo belonged to me, and that the woman had been my significant other. We both had beaming smiles, and our arms were interlocked; I was quite obviously flustered, as my ears in the photo had turned a bright scarlet. As I stared at the picture, it was all I could do to keep myself from crying. Eventually I put the photo with the note, and checked my last pocket, finding a screwdriver with a red grooved handle. Finally, I began my trek into the dense forest of purple leaved trees and dark teal grass.

I meandered through the forest for what felt like two hours, until I finally found a dirt road; the road seemed to cut straight through the forest, the expansive mass of trees continuing on the other side. The path was lined with small, grey stones. The soil of the road had no give. I looked up, for the first time able to fully see the sky above; it was of a light cyan, and as clear as could be. I was comforted by the normalcy of it. So, with no other path to follow. I began my long walk along the road; ignoring the growing hunger in my stomach as I went.

I traveled the road as long as I could, about 8 hours, before I finally had to acknowledge the pain in my gut. I needed food. I stepped off of the beaten path that I had been following, and made sure to walk in as straight of a line as I could through the woods. In a fairly short amount of time I wandered across two different types of berry bushes. The first had long, twisting, thorny brambles, and a sparse number of yellow-green leaves; the berries that it was bearing were painted an electric blue. The second bush was more akin to a very short purple oak. Its branches were straight and smooth, the plentiful leaves lilac in color, and the berries of a deep crimson. I do not know for what reason, but, I was immediately drawn to the bright blue berries. So, I moved my hand to the thorny brambles, plucked a berry from its branches, and ate it. Finding the taste quite satisfactory, and not becoming ill, I proceeded to eat more.

After eating a number of berries nearing eighteen, and pocketing a good 20, I left the bush plucked dry, and returned to the road; finding it easier to walk now that I had eaten.

I traveled the road until the sun began to set; at which point I set out into the woods to gather fallen branches. Along the way I had stopped by a small lake for a drink, and found a sort of dark blue-grey stone jutting out of it. Something in the back of my head told me it'd be useful, so I picked it up, and continued to the road. Quickly gathering a pile of wood, and some dead leaves as tinder, I arranged some stones from the side of the road into a fire pit. I took the blue-grey stone, struck it against the shaft of my screwdriver, and watched as the sparks lit a flame amongst the pile of leaves and wood.

I laid down next to the fire as the sun went below the horizon; and, feeling the warmth of the flame, gently drifted off to sleep.

Chapter 2

I woke up the next morning bright and early, the sky still painted a blend of deep purple and orange. I found the fire pit cleaned up, and all of the stones I had used back in their proper places along the road. Yes, I thought it odd. No, I did not really care that it had happened. This world is strange; I had decided the night before not to question that fact. I picked myself up off of the ground, checked the area for any hot ash, and continued along the path.

Three hours passed. I had been walking the road; only stopping to gather food and drink, and to dispose of the waste the previously mentioned activity brought about. My feet were sore, I could feel the blisters forming as my heels rubbed against the back of my shoes, and my sanity was starting to drain away. Would the same not happen to you if your only conversational partner had been yourself for two days?

My gaze was aimed at the road below me;

I had been trying to entertain myself by picking out impurities in the dirt. Needless to say, I had completely forgotten about the notebook in my jacket pocket. I was, once again, looking down at the road; this was the only reason I saw the note. A piece of paper, tinted to the color of cream, with an odd symbol branded onto the front in dark blue ink. I picked it from the ground and opened it. It read as such:

"Good job! Most people from your world kill themselves on the first day, or don't make a fire and walk along the path in the dark. (Bad idea.) Your sanity seems, and I emphasize seems, to be in the green. Also, congrats on actually understanding how to use your environment to your advantage. (Most go for the red berries instead of the blue.) You have earned yourself some more hints as to who you are. You should hurry Victor, your children are worried.
P.S. That notebook contains your life's work. -C."

I immediately pocketed the note, nearly crumpling it as I forced it into the same pocket as my notebook. I pulled the book out of my pocket at a similar speed; as I flipped through it, I found the pages filled to their brims with notes, equations, sketches, and instructions. My mind began to slowly comprehend each and every little line. I was thrilled; I finally knew something for certain. Then I remembered the note. My thoughts were simple: the person who wrote the note, C, knows all of my actions; he seems to be of a cruel wit as well; and finally, there were more people that came before me. As I continued down the road, I pondered how the others came to this place; was it a machine that brought them here too? I still don't know; and, because of the situation I am in now, I fear that question will remain forever unanswered.

I walked for a while, ate some berries, then replicated my actions of the night before. However, I could not find the comfort of sleep. Do not mistake my words; I was extremely tired, but, I found myself trapped in conscious thought. So, I decided to read through my notebook by the fire. "At least," I thought aloud, "I may learn something from my discomfort." So, I read until sleep finally arrived.

Chapter 3

The next morning was very similar to the last in that, when I woke up, I found something had changed; however, this change was not so minor as the last. You see, when I woke up, I was no longer in the forest. I had been transported to the middle of a desert in my sleep. Before then I had been finding ponds, and drinking out of those to keep hydrated. Needless to say, I was horrified, mystified, and terrified. As far as I knew, there was no water for kilometers in any direction; not to mention the fact that I had no clue how I had gotten there. I glanced around frantically, my gaze eventually meeting the dirt beneath my feet.

On the ground was a grey bottle with a black tip. Attached to the bottle was another note; there was a symbol written in red ink on the front. The note read as such:

"You need to keep that little body of yours hydrated. This bottle will last you five days if you ration it well enough; which should be long enough for you to escape the desert. (With the combined efforts of the road and yourself, of course.) P.S. Think. -C.W."

My first thought was of the knowledge I had just gained; that being the fact that there are two forces in this strange world. I knew for sure that one was hoping to see my success; only now do I realize my flaw in trusting both.

I plucked the water bottle from the dirt, and continued walking; drinking a small amount of water every two hours. I had walked for eight hours that day; I stopped five times in those eight hours, each time because I had gotten tired. Needless to say, the process was ineffective and grueling.

The heat of the desert sun beat down on my head as I trudged on throughout the day; the pouring sweat was how I discovered I had thick hair, much thicker than it was in the picture. Sometime within the third hour I had taken off my jacket and began using it as a sweat rag. After the eighth hour I fell over onto the road, and I passed out.

I woke up in the inky black of the night,

nothing to light my surroundings. I could feel the road moving beneath me; slinking and writhing its way forward. I felt lucky I hadn't gone the opposite direction, I would've never made any progress if I had.

My mind traveled back to the first note left to me; a pit formed in my stomach as I recalled the warning of travelling in the dark at night. The thoughts of what might occur raced through my head. I thought it possible that I'd only be killed if I moved; so, I kept perfectly still. Luckily the night was cold and my mind was groggy, so I once again found the comfort of sleep.

It was at that point I made a mental note to never fall asleep during the day, and to never stay up past dark with no source of light at hand.

Nothing truly interesting happened during the three following days; except my finding another bottle of water, which was filled halfway, when I had ran out the day before. So, I shall skip ahead to my fifth day in the desert.

Chapter 4

I had woken up early in the morning; the cold air a relief from the desert heat, and the sun only peeking over the horizon. I had run out of water for the second time just the day before, and had been hoping to find a third bottle lying on the path as I trudged along.

There wasn't one.

Nor any food for my consumption, as I had run out during my second day. Needless to say, I was terribly hungry; I could hear my stomach crying out in desperation for some sort of nutrition. Whilst I found no food and no water, I did find another note from C.W. on the ground. It read as such:

"Just keep walking; you're almost out of the grasp of this horrible desert. Don't stop for any reason. I promise that you will be fine if you just keep walking.
P.S. Keep thinking. -C.W."

I pocketed the note, just like all the others, and did as C.W. said. I walked.

During the two days prior I had been holding my jacket over my head as a shield from the sun's merciless rays; this allowed me to walk much longer than I would usually be able to under such conditions. It was still grueling and monotonous, as is the price for survival.

I walked for hours on end without ever stopping once; it was a surprisingly painful experience. I was starving, dehydrated, beaten on by the intense heat of my surroundings, and I refused to let my legs stop their same mechanical motion for hours. This agony continued for five hours, at which point my legs collapsed out from under me and I fell to the ground. My legs no longer willing to support me, I began to crawl along the dirt road using my arms. This continued for two hours. At the end of the second hour I found a note on the ground. I flipped it open with my left hand and began to read. The note had the following written on it:

"Hey Vic, old buddy old pal, aren't you thirsty? Wouldn't you like some water? Look to your right. -C."

I, unwittingly, did as the note said and turned my head to the right; and there it was, the most beautiful sight imaginable to any person in such a situation.

An oasis.

I mustered up as much strength as I possibly could, summoned it all to my legs, stood up, and walked.

If there is anything I know about my life, it is this: that was the most strenuous and painful experience that I have ever gone through. It felt as if the muscles in my legs were tearing with each step, like bands of rubber being overextended and snapping back into place over and over. It was torture. It took ten minutes to reach the oasis, a small pond surrounded by vibrant plant life ranging from scarlet trees to berry bushes. As soon as I got to the oasis I took off my coat, which I had been wearing so as to avoid losing it during my long crawl, and dunked my head into the water.

It felt amazing.

I drank; I ate berries and large, hard fruits; I filled my water bottles; and I relaxed. That is, until I found another note.

It had been about half an hour since I had reached the oasis, and I felt fairly energized; I was no longer in pain, to say the least. I retrieved the note from the stone it was sitting on, and opened it; I believed it would be some sort of letter of congratulations. I was wrong. So very, very wrong.

The note read as such:

"Good luck getting back. -C."

I dropped the note in horror, and frantically glanced around in every direction. The road was gone. I ran away from the oasis, about twelve feet out to scan for any semblance of the road, only to turn around and find it gone. It was gone. The oasis was gone. Everything went wrong all at once. I hadn't picked up my water bottles before rushing to try and find any hint of the road.

I was stranded in a desert with no water, no food, and no road. I didn't know what to do. So, I ran.

I just ran.

I ran as fast as I could, and as far as I could. I ran day and night for two days through the barren desert. I found you on the second day.

I found the forest. I collapsed against you, and I'm too weary to pick myself back up.

I'm going to die here against a purple oak.

————

Victor then pulled the picture from his breast pocket, shifting around the letters left for him during his journey; now yellowed and wrinkled from the sun.

"I will never know who I was."

Caitlin Diener
Fort Walton Beach High School
10th Grade, Amy Holt

The Void

Standing, waiting at the edge
    Of the cliff
Shadows filling the bright shine,
    Filling the world, a dark void
A smooth voice, a whispered one
    calling silently, careful not to be heard
The tiny fingertips at the edge
    of her mind
      voices as hands, beckoning
An enemy in the clouds,
    waiting to attack
The whispers floating through the air
    Dark, dangerous
      quiet, yet screaming
A stranger is waiting
    (To attack?)
     (Or to help?)
    Waiting for the void to be filled
The shadows push through, wanting to win
    But the void is not filled
      The light is too strong

Brianna Gavenda

Fort Walton Beach High School
10th Grade, Amy Holt

Drowning

The water has a light blue color, so clear I can see
the rows of sand at the bottom
The fish swim carelessly, tormenting me with a
trait I always lacked
The white caps carry the promise of taking away
any pain I've ever had to endure, so I listen
The water pulls me in reminding me of a gentle
caress, slowly taking away every memory that's
ever weighed me down
The first minute I kick my legs struggling to keep
my head above water
The second minute I feel the burning sensation
coming up my spine making its way down my
arms and flowing through my legs
The third minute I go under, and it's in this exact
moment I realize what bliss feels like
The fourth minute my head feels like it's gonna
explode with the lack of air
The fifth minute I open my mouth welcoming the
swirls into my lungs, it becomes my air
The sixth minute I am gone

Anne Marie Willis
Fort Walton Beach High School
11th Grade, Amy Holt

That Dragon Hubris

Once upon a time there was a village in the woods. This village was plagued by monsters and the villagers could never seem to escape from their nightmarish claws. In fact, many years before this, a ferocious dragon that called itself Hubris had terrorized the land but had since disappeared. One day a mighty hero stumbled upon the village, claiming he was the answer to all their problems. The villagers, seeing his might, begged him to stay, offering him a home so long as he would protect the village. The hero agreed to stay and fight. Soon enough the people of the settlement worshipped him. This praise caused the warrior to grow prideful, and after a particularly easy battle he confidently proclaimed that he was undefeatable and that even that mythical dragon was too weak to stop him. Within days of his proclamation the dragon of legend descended upon the village. The cause of the dragon's sudden appearance was unknown to the villagers but the terror it should have invoked was obvious. Despite the dragons terrifying stature and ground shaking roar the people were unfazed. They proudly proclaimed that their mightiest warrior would defeat the dragon with ease. Even the hero himself seemed unafraid as he lumbered up to the beast without even the barest amount of armor. The dragon merely huffed a hot breath of smoke at his approach. "Tell me," the mighty dragon grumbled to the villagers "who called me here?" Suddenly there was a loud cry and the dragon whipped around to find a small child, "How dare you challenge our mightiest hero!" the child continued to curse it as the other villagers joined in. "Boastful villagers do you not understand?!" the dragon roared, seething as its eyes bore into the crowd "I am your destruction! Be ready to fight by sunrise or die." And with that the dragon took off into the blazing sky. The villagers promptly turned to their warrior, only to find him cowering at the thought of his own demise. Not realizing his fear they rallied around him; claiming that someone as strong as him would defeat the dragon easily. So the next day as he faced the dragon he fought with renewed pride, even managing to strike the dragon in its eye. Though he fought well his arrogance was surely the end of him and when he made a too-bold move the dragon set him ablaze, extinguishing him and his pride within moments. The rest of the village could only look on in abject horror as the dragon began its rampage. And when the last villager fell the dragon merely grinned with satisfaction and flew away, back to the humble cave from which it had been stirred.

The End

Anna Henry

Fort Walton Beach High School
10th Grade, Amy Holt

Same Self, Different Mind

The corners of my memory, A little girl standing
by the window on one side
The corners of the house of my youth. I remember
that time The girl that was So much taller than
me, When she led me, I longed for you when, I
turned my face up to you When I hugged you
With your child hands
The feet that only pattered where my little feet
went
I didn't know your meaning then, At that time I
was happy only dreaming

I remember that time near the end of elementary
school. When my height finally became taller than
your height. But at that point I neglected you, The
you I had wished for, The memory of your face
Became distorted and forgotten, And in my mind
where the thought of you was dust piled up. And
your neglected appearance, I didn't know it back
then, But your meaning was that wherever I am
You will also be
Protecting that space, Perhaps that was why I
didn't know it was the end

Don't go like this you say: Even if I go, don't
worry, Because you'll do well on your own I
think of the first time I met you, And at some
point you just became so big
You put a period on our relationship but Don't be
sorry towards me And whatever form I take, You
will see me again, Please let us meet happily at
that time.

I remember that time when I darkly forgot. When
I met you again I was 13 years old
I awkwardly hugged you again, For a moment.
Even though I was gone for a long time, You took
me in again Without any repulsion, Without you I
am nothing
As the dawn passed, us two Greeted the morning.
Don't let go of my hand forever Because I won't
let go of you either. I remember that time at the
beginning of my teens, I let you go, that's right, I
saw no Further than my nose And I let you leave
That time, crying and laughing, Those moments
Alone When I was with you
Those were the happiest I've ever been, And now
they're only memories
Clutching my smashed heart, I said it, That I
wouldn't be able to do this anymore
But every time I wanted to give up You said, from
next to me: Kid, you really can do it. That's right,
I remember. When I had fallen into the pit of
Hopelessness and despair I pushed you away,
Even when I wanted to meet you, You firmly
stayed by my side, Even if I didn't ask for it. So
because of that, stay with me. Because I won't let

go of you, A second time. There was my birth and then there was the end of my life. You protected both of those things. The corners of my memory, A little girl standing by the window on one side. The corners of the house of my youth.

Alison Janetis
Fort Walton Beach High School
9th Grade, Amy Holt

Lil' Blue

Oh lil' Blue, what a wonderful life you have
Your soul is Pure, wings-stretched for flight-
And song Riveting, Beautiful like the hue you
wear.

Your eyes a charming view over vacant love-
Song like Cadence for the empty-
Song like courage-strength-to the faint hearts of
hopeless.

Oh lil' Blue, what a wonderful life you have
The Old-skeptical and jealous- of the life you live
Will your vision stay so optimistic of the
purgatory?

The dark false corrupt-impure-sphere
Will it put away your burnish light?
Taint and clip your delicate wings?

Oh lil' Blue, May you mature with the old soul
clasped within!
May your persona hold blazing, vivid, intense!
Never conforming to the interfering Monsters-
Let it be as graceful and grand as now's contents.

Oh lil' Blue, what my message and guidance
sends is-
You lil' Blue-
Were meant to be a dazzling fluorescent
Oh lil' Blue, never fade to the color of your name
Because you are a dazzling fluorescent!

Abigail Coyle
Fort Walton Beach High School
11th Grade, Amy Holt

What Kind of Habit Is This?

They said they finally broke the myth.
That it takes 21 days to break a habit.
They called 90 the new magic number.
I'm 106 days late and counting.
On day 91 I expected to hear a pitter patter
coming down the hall as I opened the door.
On day 92 I woke up expecting my best friend to
be beside me.
On day 93 I'm one more day away from the last
time I hugged her yet I can still feel her fur
tickling my skin.
On day 95 I mention her as if she was still home
waiting on me like always
On day 96, 97, 98 she is still with me in theory
It feels like there's a vacant hole inside of me my
brain keeps trying to fill
But that doesn't make her heart start beating
That doesn't change the fact I still look for her
when I'm scared
And my mind shoots straight to her when I'm
home alone
That a crinkling bag can open up a tidal wave of
emotions
I constantly remind myself she is gone.

Getting told how stupid it is to love an animal so
much; they don't live as long as us
An animal that was my only friend for most of
my life
The sister I was never given
We grew up together
Day 170 I wrote on my paper that I had a pet
Erasing it slowly I felt a burn rising in my
stomach shooting to my heart.
Severing my connection to feel anything real and
left me with this hollow pain.
So that nothing felt real and the chair disappeared
becoming a cloud.
However my cloud was made of thunder and
lightning.
My cloud stabbed and struck until I could no
longer stand to be.
Falling down in heavy raindrops.
Staining everything with memory.
I become lost and stranded on my own island.
Because time moves on and I refuse to
My entire world stopped in a beat.
As soon as they said two words, "She's gone"
So tell me, what kind of habit is this?

Made in the USA
Middletown, DE
06 December 2018